This book belongs to
my friend:

Grace

A NOTE TO PARENTS

In *Little Bill's Big Choice*, Little Bill is faced with a common preschool dilemma: When you are invited to two simultaneous events, what should you do? Read the story to follow Little Bill through each step of his decision-making process.

Making choices, solving problems, and being sensitive to other people's feelings are difficult skills to learn, especially when they are all combined in one challenging situation. As you read, talk about why Little Bill has so much trouble deciding what to do. Does he worry about letting his friends down? Ask your child what she would do if she were in Little Bill's shoes. Remind her of a time when she had to make a similar tough choice and how she handled it.

One of the most important things parents can do for their children is to listen. Like Little Bill's family members and friends, be available to offer encouragement and kindness when needed. Do not make all of your child's choices for her, but provide guidance. As she grows and experiences new life situations, chat often about what she is thinking and feeling. Even if she does not always show it, she will appreciate knowing that she can turn to you at any time.

Learning Fundamental: 💬 **social skills**

For more parent and kid-friendly activities, go to www.nickjr.com.

Little Bill's Big Choice

Published by Scholastic Inc., 90 Old Sherman Turnpike, Danbury, CT 06816

ISBN 0-7172-6636-2

Printed in the U.S.A.

First Scholastic Printing, May 2003

Little Bill's Big Choice

by
Kitty Fross

illustrated by
Jennifer Oxley

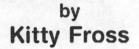

SCHOLASTIC INC.

New York Toronto London Auckland Sydney
Mexico City New Delhi Hong Kong Buenos Aires

One morning before school, Little Bill heard the telephone ringing.

"Little Bill, you have a phone call," his mother called. "It's your friend Monty!"

Little Bill hurried downstairs and picked up
the telephone.

A minute later, Little Bill hung up the phone and ran to find his mother. "Guess what, Mama?" he said breathlessly. "Monty has an extra ticket for the baseball game tomorrow! Can I go with him?"

Little Bill's mother reached for her calendar. "That sounds wonderful, Little Bill, but aren't you going on a picnic with Kiku tomorrow?"

Little Bill's face fell. "Oh, no. That's right!" he said. "I really want to go to the ball game with Monty. But I really want to have a picnic with Kiku, too!"

Little Bill's mother nodded. "Well, baby," she said, "I guess you're going to have to make a choice."

"Which should I choose?" Little Bill asked his mother. "That's up to you," she answered. "But you already said 'yes' to Kiku, and I'm sure you don't want to disappoint her."

"That's true," said Little Bill. "But I don't want to disappoint Monty, either!"

"As long as you're honest with your friends, I'm sure they'll understand," his mother said. "Now we'd better hurry, or you'll be late for school!"

"I wish I could go to the ball game and the picnic,"
Little Bill thought to himself as he walked to school.

"If there were two of me, I could do both!"

Soon Little Bill arrived at school.

Kiku saw him and waved cheerfully. "Hi, Little Bill! I can't wait for our picnic tomorrow," she called.

Little Bill waved back, but he couldn't think of anything to say. A funny nervous feeling in his stomach was making all his words go away.

All day in school, Little Bill thought about what he should do. Every time he looked at Kiku, the strange nervous feeling came back. "I don't know what to do," he thought to himself. "I have to choose, but how do I choose between my friends?"

Finally near the end of the school day, Kiku walked over to Little Bill. "Little Bill, you're acting funny," she said. "What's the matter?"

Little Bill gulped. Then he remembered what his mother had said about being honest.

Little Bill took a deep breath, and then his words came tumbling out. "It's just that Monty invited me to a baseball game tomorrow," he told Kiku. "I want to go on a picnic with you, but I don't want to disappoint Monty."

Little Bill continued, "I can't do both at the same time, and there's only one of me, so I have to choose!" The words kept rushing out until he had told Kiku everything.

Kiku was quiet for a moment. "A baseball game is really special, Little Bill," she said at last. "We could go on a picnic anytime."

Little Bill smiled. "But Kiku, a picnic is special, too!" he said. And just like that, he knew what he would do. "I don't want to miss the picnic," he said. "Maybe Monty and I can go to a ball game some other time."

Walking home from school, Little Bill told his great-grandmother, Alice the Great, about his day. "Kiku asked me first, so I'm going to the picnic," he explained. "But now I have to tell Monty I can't go to the game."

Alice the Great looked thoughtful. "Little Bill," she said, "are you sure there's no way you can do both?"

At home, Little Bill thought about what his great-grandmother had said. "Well, I can't be in two places at the same time," he said slowly.

"That's true," Alice the Great agreed. "But can you be in two places at two different times?" She winked at Little Bill. "Think it over," she encouraged. "Maybe there's a great idea just waiting to jump into your head."

Little Bill thought hard. "Hmm. Two places at two different times . . . " Suddenly his face lit up. "Alice the Great, will you help me call Kiku's house?" he asked. "I don't think I have to choose at all!"

Alice the Great dialed Kiku's number.

"Hi, Kiku," Little Bill said. "I have an idea. Could we have our picnic after the baseball game?"

"Sure, Little Bill," Kiku said. "Hey, I just had an idea, too!"

The next afternoon, Little Bill and Monty sat in the stands with Monty's grandmother, watching their favorite baseball team.

"The Blue Sox are the best! They're going to win!" Little Bill yelled happily.

Monty and Little Bill waved their banners.
"Go-o-o-o-o, Blue Sox!" they cheered as loud
as they could.

After the game, they drove to the park, where Kiku and her grandmother were waiting.

"Thanks for inviting me to your picnic," Monty said as he ate his hot dog.

"Yeah, that was a great idea, Kiku! And thanks for taking me to the game, Monty," Little Bill said happily. "I'm so glad I got to choose both of you!"